to

_____

from

_____

To Lucie, Emily and James A.A.

Text by Lois Rock
Illustrations copyright © 2004 Alex Ayliffe
This edition copyright © 2006 Lion Hudson

The moral rights of the author and illustrator
have been asserted

A Lion Children's Book
an imprint of
Lion Hudson plc
Mayfield House, 256 Banbury Road,
Oxford OX2 7DH, England
www.lionhudson.com
ISBN-13: 978-0-7459-6026-5
ISBN-10: 0-7459-6026-X

First edition 2004
This edition 2006
1 3 5 7 9 10 8 6 4 2 0

A catalogue record for this book is
available from the British Library

Typeset in Baskerville BT
Printed and bound in China

my very first

Bedtime

book

Words by
Lois Rock

Pictures by
Alex Ayliffe

LION
CHILDREN'S

Contents

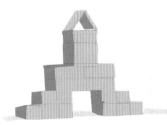

The Sandcastle Game

It was the day of the outing. Everyone had packed their beach things. They had climbed on a bus.

They had come a long way down to the seaside.

"It's a very little beach," said
Paul. He felt a bit disappointed.

"Don't worry," said Debbie. She was one of the helpers. "The tide is still going out. The beach will get bigger.

"I think everyone should play in the sea while it's so near," she added.

So they did. What a splash they made.

After a while, they all felt hungry.
They came running back up the
beach to where the picnic was ready.

"That was a long run," puffed Paul.
"The beach is enormous."

They had all kinds of delicious things
to eat.

After that, they hunted in rockpools
near the cliffs. They saw baby crabs
and darting shrimps and tiny fish.

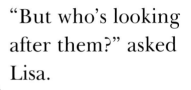

"But who's looking
after them?" asked
Lisa.

"The sea comes back
every day and fills the pools,"
said Debbie. "These pools are
a safe place for the little ones."

Then Debbie had an idea. "Let's build sandcastles," she said. "When the sea comes back, we can see whose sandcastle lasts longest."

Lisa built an enormous castle with wet sand that gurgled as they dug.

Sam packed damp sand into buckets, then tipped it out to make towers.

Paul thought hard. He found a slab of
rock high up the beach and began to
build on it.

It was hard work. His sand was dry,
and he had to go and fetch water in
a bucket to make it stick together.

Then they played games with bats and
balls. Slowly the sea began to roll in.

First it reached Lisa's castle. It lasted
a long time because it was so big.

Then the sea came up to Sam's castle.
"Oh," they said, as it sank in the
waves. "It was so lovely."

Then the sea came up to Paul's castle. The waves washed all around the rock. They splashed the castle. But they didn't come high enough to knock it down.

"Well done, Paul," said Debbie. "You chose the best place." She put a seaweed flag on the sandcastle.

Then it was time for everyone to go home. "Goodbye, beach!" they all shouted.

The flag on Paul's sandcastle was still there, and it waved back to them.

Bless the shore
and bless the sea;
God bless you
and God bless me.

Bless the sea
and bless the shore;
keep us safe
for evermore.

When Lion Gave a Party

Lion was special.
He lived on the special
window corner. All the
toys knew it was the
very best place to sit.

So when Lion sent his great friend Mouse over to the toy cupboard with party invitations, everyone was very excited.

"Oh, this is for me," said Plush Bear. "I knew Lion was going to ask me to his party."

"And this one's for me," said Velvet Cat.

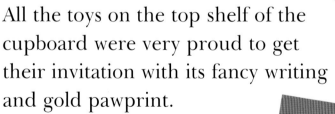

All the toys on the top shelf of the cupboard were very proud to get their invitation with its fancy writing and gold pawprint.

"Doesn't it make you feel special," purred Velvet Cat.

The next day, a wonderful feast
was prepared in the window
corner. There were platefuls
of food and bright balloons
and little tiny gifts.

Just before party time,
Mouse climbed high onto
the window frame and
blew a shiny trumpet.
"The party is about to
begin," he cried.

Velvet Cat was dozing. She heard the shout. "Oh, how tiresome," she meowed. "I'm sleeping."

Plush Bear looked up from a box. "Grandma has sent me some new clothes," he said. "I have to try them on."

And then all the toys began to make excuses.

Mouse told Lion, and Lion (who had heard anyway) growled in a rather dangerous kind of way.

"They don't want to come?" he said. "But the party is all ready. I can't let everything go to waste."

Lion narrowed his eyes. He always did when he was thinking. "Go back to the toy cupboard," he said to Mouse, "and ask the other toys… the ones who are all jumbled up on the bottom shelf. Tell them to come to my party."

The jumbled-up toys looked very odd.
Knitted Rabbit had lost an eye. Softie
the Clown was so floppy he couldn't
stand up. Easter Chick was covered
in chocolate marks. But they all
smiled big smiles and hurried to
Lion's party.

"Thank you for asking us," they said. "Mostly we get forgotten. This is such a treat."

Lion was happy. He whispered to Mouse, "We have so much food, you must go and make sure everyone who wants to come is invited."

So Mouse went to the box next to the cupboard and told even the old toys to come: the forgotten toys, the battered toys, the outgrown toys. Everyone who came had a wonderful time.

Dear God,
Bless all my friends,
especially the ones I sometimes forget.

The Wildflower Garden

All the children enjoyed playing in the park—on the swings and everything else.

Sometimes they stopped to watch the people who came to clear a patch of brambly ground nearby.

One day a sign went up.
"Now we know what they're
doing," said the grown-ups.

They were turning the old
bramble patch into a wildflower
garden that would be a
lovely place for butterflies and
birds. That day they needed
help to sow the seeds.

The lady in charge had a huge
sack of all kinds of wildflower seeds,
and she used a scoop to fill little
bags for the children.

"Just go and scatter
them over the ground
that we've raked
smooth," she said.

The children set off, flinging handfuls
of seed wherever they liked.

Some of the seeds fell
by the edge of the patch,
where there were lots of
stones.

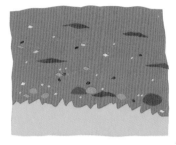

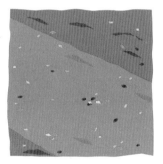

Some of the seeds fell on
the little paths that had
been rolled hard and flat.

Some of the seeds fell into
the brambles far beyond.

Most of the seeds fell
on good brown earth.

When all the sowing was done,
everyone stayed to admire the work.

"Look," said Melissa. "The birds like
the seeds already."

It was true. On the hard paths, the birds were gobbling up all the seeds that they could find.

"Never mind," said the lady in charge. "It's just beginning to rain. Now the rest of the seeds will sink a little into the soil and begin to grow."

There were rainy days
and sunny days.

No one ever knew if the
seeds that fell among the
brambles grew, because
the sun and the rain
made the brambles
grow even faster.

The seeds grew quite quickly around the stony edges.

Then one very hot day, they all began to droop.

"They can't grow strong roots in all those stones," explained Melissa's mother. "Let's watch what happens to the seedlings in the good soil."

In the good soil, the seeds grew and grew. The children ran along the paths to see the butterflies that danced from flower to flower. And later, when the flowers turned to seedheads, birds came and found hundreds and thousands of seeds to eat.

Bless the seeds and bless the soil
and bless the sun and rain.
Bless the leaves and bless the flowers;
bring harvest once again.

The Not-Quite Twins

Joanna and Joanna were not twins. Not at all. They just went to the same playgroup. They just had the same name...

the same sort of hair, the same
fondness for pink and purple, and
they were both very good at painting.

Everyone called them the not-quite twins, and that upset both of them.

"Because the other Joanna is really naughty," said the Joanna whose best toy was a clean white bear.

"Because the other Joanna is a goody-goody," said the Joanna whose best toy was a gold-brown bear with muddy marks.

One day after painting, the teacher asked them to wash out the jars and brushes.

"Yes, Miss Mackie," said Joanna, smiling sweetly.

"I don't want to," sulked Joanna.
"I want to go and play outside
now."

And she stomped off and walked
out with her coat over her head.

Miss Mackie went to chat with the mothers. While she wasn't looking, Joanna went and washed her hands very carefully. Then she dried them on a clean towel.

She didn't wash out any jars or brushes as she said she would.

She just scampered off to
fetch her clean white bear
and play ballerinas.

Joanna looked out from under her coat. She felt sad. She had been very grumpy. And she hadn't been fair to kind Miss Mackie.

So she crept back into the classroom. She washed out her brushes and her jar of water.

Then she fetched her gold-brown
bear. He looked at her. She knew
what he must be thinking.

"Oh, all right, Bear," she said. "But
you'll have to come and help."

Together they washed out the other
brushes and the other jars.

Soon it was storytime. "Before I begin," said Miss Mackie, "I want to say thank you to the helpful people who tidied up as I asked."

And then the not-quite twins knew just how different they were!

Bless me when I am grumpy.
Bless me when I am good.
Help me be kind
as others are kind
and do all the things I should.

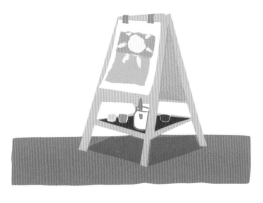

The World's Tallest Tower

Daniel and Katy both wanted to play with the building blocks.

"I want to build the tallest tower in all the world!" shouted Katy. "So I need lots and lots of blocks."

She grabbed the big box of blocks
and the middle box of blocks
and the little box of blocks.

Daniel was left with the cracked box
of blocks, and everyone knew that the
cracked box had only plain blocks in it.

Katy had all the best blocks: red
and yellow, blue and green, pink
and purple.

She had squares and rectangles and
triangles, pillars and arches and turrets.

She began to build a huge tower right
in the middle of the big green mat.
"My castle!" she shouted.

Daniel stood in a little corner, looking
at his box of blocks and thinking.

"See how quickly I'm making mine," boasted Katy. All the children came to watch as she arranged the biggest blocks on the mat and began building the walls.

In his corner, Daniel was counting out his blocks. He put them in groups: squares and rectangles and planks.

He was still thinking. Only Jennifer came to watch, and she soon got bored watching someone who was just thinking.

"Now look at what I'm doing,"
shrieked Katy. "Now I'm doing a row
of pillars with arches in between, and
all the blocks go in the right order all
the way around.

"And on top of that goes another row,
and then I'll do more and more
till it's as tall as me."

Daniel had done just one row,
with one doorway marked.

The children were still watching Katy.

"When will you put the turrets on?" asked Josh.

"They go on last," said Katy, "you should know that. I know all about towers."

But there was a problem. The tower wasn't nearly as tall as Katy, and the top row was only half made. The turrets were the only pieces left in the boxes.

Josh began to giggle, and everyone else just went away whispering.

"Come over here," said Jennifer. "Look!"

In the corner, Daniel's tower was
perfect. And he had carefully
used every single block he had.

Bless the things I make and do.
May I build them strong and true.

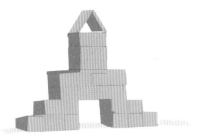

Jamie's Frog Friend

Of all the toys in the world, Jamie most liked frogs. He had more frogs than anyone: little frogs, big frogs and medium-sized jumping frogs.

"And they're all my friends," he said.

When Jamie went to bed he always took with him a big green cuddly frog: Frogo.

"My best friend in all the world," said Jamie.

So when the day came for Jamie
to begin going to playgroup, he
had a problem.

"Frogo has to come," said Jamie.
"But I can't leave the others
behind either."

His mother sighed. Then she fetched one of her bags. "The frogs will like green," she said.

Jamie packed all the frogs.

"There's still space for more," he said, as he and his mother walked to playgroup. "So I can have more frogs."

"Maybe," said his mother.

The playgroup leader was called Beth.
She loved Jamie's frogs. She found a
chair just the right size for Frogo.

"Come and join the circle now," said
Beth. "Find out what we're going to
do today."

Jamie didn't want to.
He sat with Frogo.
A girl came and
shook Frogo's
hand shyly.

Jamie didn't go out to play with the others. He sat on a green beanbag and talked to all his frogs. "I'm talking to my friends," he said to Beth.

Jamie didn't want to go to playgroup
ever again. His mother bought him a
new frog—just like Frogo, only tiny.
She said its name was Frogotini and
it loved going out. But Jamie knew
that Frogotini was just something
to make him go to playgroup
without the rest of his
frog friends.

That morning he sat in the circle of
boys and girls, clutching Frogotini. The
shy girl used her little finger to shake
Frogotini's tiny hand.

"Today we are going on a nature
walk," said Beth. "Everyone must
wear their outdoor things."

Jamie stomped along miserably. He didn't see anything. He didn't hear anything. Not until the shy girl, called Em, shouted at him, "Jamie, come here!"

Beth led him to where Em
was pointing. "Look!" she said.

It was a real live frog, as
green as the leaves by the
pond. It tried to look at Jamie
bravely, but he could see it was
trembling and scared.

"Hello, Frog," whispered Jamie.
"Will you be my friend?"

The frog blinked back.
Then it gave Jamie a
little wink and jumped
into the pond.

After that, Jamie's other frogs didn't seem quite so real. "I still like them," he said, "but I like them because they're toys. They're not real friends."

"And what about the frog in the pond?" asked his mother. "Is he a real friend?"

"No," giggled Jamie. "He's a real frog."

"So who is a real friend?" asked his mother.

"Em," said Jamie.

God bless all those that I love.
God bless all those that love me.
God bless all those that love those
   that I love,
and all those that love those that
   love me.

From an old New England sampler

Playground Games

"Take care in the playground," said Miss James. "And take care of each other."

Everybody rushed out.

Miss James shook her head.
"I don't think everyone was
listening," she said.

Janey and Marisa and Izzy were playing
their skipping games. They could hop
and step, backwards and forwards.

Amanda was just learning how to skip
with a rope. The other three didn't
want to help her.

"Go and play by yourself," said Izzy.
She stuck her tongue out.

Amanda crept off to a
quiet corner. She tried
her best but still got
all tangled up.

Just then a big crowd of the noisiest,
biggest children came racing around.
They were playing a chasing game
with a huge red ball.

Izzy got knocked right over.
Janey and Marisa simply ran
away.

"Stop!" shouted Amanda.
"Izzy might be hurt."

Only Zak seemed to notice what she
said. He looked at Izzy, then shouted
to his friends, "Come on, let's go!"

And the gang raced off after the ball.

Amanda hurried over to Izzy and gave her a little hug. "I'll help you walk back to Miss James," she said.

Miss James had seen everything and was already running to help.

Amanda picked up Izzy's rope as well as her own and folded them neatly before taking them back inside.

Izzy's knee needed to be washed and patted dry, and then Miss James put on an enormous sticky bandage.

"Now I won't be able to play with
my rope," sobbed Izzy. "And Janey
and Marisa will get better than me."

"I can teach you to throw straight," said
Amanda. "That won't hurt your leg."

Everyone was astonished when
Amanda and Izzy did their throwing.
Amanda never missed her aim, and
Izzy was getting quite good, too.

"We want to learn," said everyone.

"I think it would be good
for everyone to share the
games they know," said
Miss James.

And so they did.

Bless all the people
we meet today.
Help us to help them
in every way.

Runaway Sue

There were so many things Sue wanted to do in a day.

She wanted to play with her toys. So she played with all her toys in her bedroom.

Then she wanted to dance. So she ran to the living room, started the music and began to dance.

She danced with her bear. She danced with the cushions. She danced over the chairs.

Then she wanted to cook.

So she ran to the kitchen.
She got out her little bowl
and spoon. Then she
tipped in some flour.
Then she added
some cocoa.

Then she poured
in some milk.

Then she sprinkled
in some sugar.

Then she began to stir.

She had a taste of the mix. It wasn't very nice, so she decided she'd like to get out her paints.

"Sue," said her mother, "I think we ought to tidy some things up before you do anything else."

"I don't want to!" shouted Sue. "I'm going out." And she ran out of the house.

In the garden she swung on the swing
and dug in the sand. She hunted for
snails and she collected pink flowers.

Then she climbed into the fork of the
big apple tree. She watched the
clouds. They were white and fluffy.

"I will stay here forever," she said to
herself.

A cloud blew across the sun. The air felt cold. Grey clouds came scurrying by.

A raindrop fell, and then another. Sue felt very unhappy. "I will have to go back to the house," she said. "And I will have to tidy up everything."

She climbed out of the tree and turned to go.

Her mother was already hurrying
down the path with a big umbrella.

"Just in time," she said, as she and Sue walked back to the kitchen. "I found your mix and I added a bit more of this and that. Now I've made it into a cake. I'm going to put icing on it, and you can go and bring all your toys to the party."

In a few minutes of being busy,
everything was right again.

Bless all our good times
and bless all our bad times
and bless all our lifetimes with love.
So may the world that we live in
each day
be as lovely as heaven above.

In a Minute

Sophie was very excited. Grandpa was coming to stay. She stayed up just past bedtime to watch him arrive.

"Hello, Grandpa! I'm so glad you've come. You will read me a story, won't you?" she said.

"In a minute," said Grandpa. "I'm just going to have something to eat."

Sophie helped get out the cups and plates and waited while Grandpa had something to eat.

"Is it time now?" she asked.

"In a minute," said Grandpa. "Your mother wants to show me the garden while there's still light to see it."

So Sophie put on her coat and pulled on her boots and went to watch.

Her mother and Grandpa looked at the
bare patch that her mother had just dug.

"Is it time for my story now?" she asked.

"In a minute," said Grandpa. "Just let me get my bags out of the car."

So Sophie put the outdoor light on to help Grandpa see. She even ran out to help him carry in one of his bags because he didn't have enough hands.

"It must be time for my story now!" she said.

"In a minute," said her mother. "In fact it's time for you to go and wash your feet. You're lucky you didn't step on anything nasty out there."

So Sophie went to the bathroom.
Her mother put some water in the
bathtub and Sophie splashed her feet
and wiggled her toes in the bubbles.

Then she dried her feet, went to fetch some fluffy socks to warm her toes up and pulled them on.

"I'm all ready for my story," she called to Grandpa.

"In a minute," said Grandpa, "I'm
in the middle of unpacking now."

"It's not fair," said Sophie sulkily.
"I keep being told to wait a minute
and now it's taking HOURS!"

"I think you should go to your bed and wait for Grandpa," said her mother, very firmly.

So Sophie went.

"How long do you think a minute is?" she asked Bear.

But before Bear could answer, Grandpa came.

"I want to read you your story," he said, "but look—I've got a new story for you as well!"

"Don't keep her up too long!" Sophie's mother called from downstairs.

"I'll be down in a minute," said Grandpa, as he and Sophie made themselves snug in the armchair.

Bless the time that goes so fast,
the time that goes so slow.
Give me lots of happy times
as through the years I go.

Cinnamon Bear

There was once a little girl called
Gemma. She loved cuddly toys.

She had one elephant,
four rabbits and
seven mice.

She had so many bears her mother
couldn't count them.

Gemma knew exactly how many
bears she had. "Thirty-nine," she
told her mother.

Gemma knew exactly where each of her cuddly toys liked to sleep. Every one of them had a special place.

So she knew at once when one of them was missing. Gemma was very upset, but she didn't have time to cry.

"I must find my lost bear," she said. "He's called Cinnamon because he's brown. He has a blue ribbon and a curly smile."

She looked everywhere in the
bedroom. Cinnamon was not there.
A tear trickled down Gemma's
cheek. "He's always been a very
mischievous bear," she sobbed.

Then she dried her eyes. She looked everywhere upstairs.

She looked everywhere downstairs.

She looked outside. There was
no Cinnamon Bear.

"We'll have to go back to
the park and check there,"
she told her mother.

Even though the stars were
beginning to twinkle in the
sky, they went out to look.

All alone, tucked into a swing,
was Cinnamon.

"Hooray!" shouted Gemma. And
she ran to cuddle him. "I love you,
Cinnamon Bear," she whispered.

"When we get home," said Gemma
to her mother, "it mustn't be bedtime
anymore. We need to have a party to
celebrate. Because Cinnamon was lost,
and now we've found him."

Everyone sat down to enjoy juice
and cookies, while outside the stars
smiled down from the sky.

Bless me when I'm feeling lost
and don't know where to go.
Bring me safely home again
to those who love me so.

Bedtime Words

bed a soft place to lie down to sleep

pillow a place to lay your head to sleep

quilt a snuggly coverlet to keep you warm in bed

teddy a soft toy to hug while you sleep

cuddle a long hug

kiss a way of saying "I love you"

dark a time when the sun shines on
the other side of the world

moon a silver light that
shines in the night-time sky

star a twinkly light that shines
in the night-time sky

dream a story you make up when
you are asleep

morning
the beginning of
another busy day